How Buffalo Lost Her Coat

Belinda Dupont

Illustrations by P G Rob

AuthorHouse™ UK
1663 Liberty Drive
Bloomington, IN 47403 USA
www.authorhouse.co.uk
Phone: 0800.197.4150

Published by AuthorHouse 04/28/2018

ISBN: 978-1-5462-8521-2 (sc)
ISBN: 978-1-5462-8520-5 (e)

Print information available on the last page.

authorHOUSE°

For my Nepali family:
Sanja, Ajamburi, Raju and Geeta

Buffalo is the gentlest and cleanest of creatures. She walks with a bit of a waddle and pokes her nose forward a long way as if she is sniffing the air.

She gives the farmer and his family creamy milk which is very good to drink. It is also made into ghee, a kind of butter. Everyone loves Buffalo. When she was a baby she had a coat of thick, wavy hair but as an adult she only has grey skin and people wonder why.

How did she lose her coat?

Well, before I tell you how she lost her coat, first I have to tell you that Buffalos live in many countries but this story comes from Nepal. Nepal is a small country in the Himalayan Mountains. These mountains are so big and steep there is very little flat land where the farmers can grow their crops. Over hundreds of years the farmers have dug into the hillsides and created flat, terraced fields. The hillsides look like huge staircases for giants to walk up over the snow-capped mountains to get to Tibet. Tibet is another country on the other side of the Himalayas.

3

The terraced fields have raised edges so the farmer can flood the fields with water to grow rice. Maize, wheat, mustard and other crops are also grown.

The farmer digs the terraces using a wooden plough that turns over the soil. The plough is pulled by a strong ox. He is a great help to the farmer. Tractors cannot be used because they are too heavy and could break down the walls of the fields.

Every morning before going to school the children go out to collect food for Buffalo and the other animals. They use a sharp, hooked knife, called a *hasya,* to cut some of the weeds and grasses that grow at the edges of the fields. They also climb trees to cut some leaves so the animals will have a good variety of things to eat.

The heavy load is carried home by the children in cone-shaped baskets called *dokos*. The *doko* rests on the child's back and is supported by a *namlo* band around their forehead. Adults carry loads this way too.

At the farm Buffalo and her companions, the ox and goats, are very happy to see the children bringing them their breakfast.

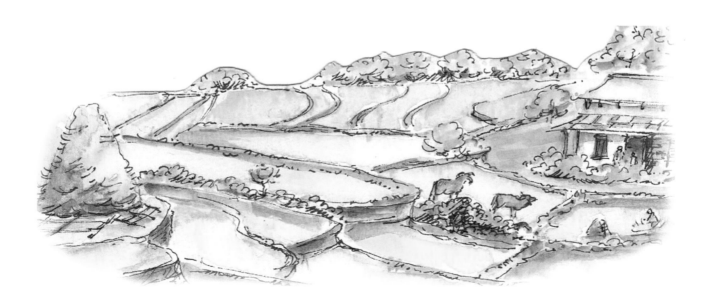

When Buffalo gives birth to her beautiful
baby she spends a lot of time licking its
thick, wavy coat. Her tough tongue
massages the calf so it can grow
big and strong and healthy.

Scientists have given Buffalo a lovely name, *Bubalus bubalis*. She is also called a water buffalo because she loves to spend part of her day wallowing in the waterhole. I told you she is clean but she also loves to get muddy because the mud keeps her skin in good condition. When she is back at the farm she shades herself from the sun under a shelter or a tree.

The children of Nepal ask why Buffalo has grey skin instead of a long, hairy coat like her calf. They also ask why she walks along with her neck and head stretched out as if she is sniffing the air and looking for something. This is the story they are told.

Tibetan traders came over the mountains to Nepal to buy goods that couldn't be made in their country. Even though it was summer they wore thick woollen boots, hats and heavy coats because high up in the mountains it is cold and snow-covered all year round.

sacks of spices

They were delighted to find wonderful goods to buy in Nepal. They bought barrels, brass pots and boxes, rolls of cloth, tools and carpets. In fact they bought so much there was more than they could carry themselves. They realised they would need help to carry everything back over the mountains to Tibet.

Then one of them had a good idea. 'Let's ask the gentle Buffalo if she will help us,' he said. They all agreed and went to speak to her.

Buffalo was very polite and shook her head. 'Kind sirs,' she replied, 'thank you for asking me but I'm sorry, I need to bathe each day. How will I find water high up there where it has all turned to snow and ice? I cannot help you. Please ask someone else.'

The traders looked unhappy. Buffalo did want to help in some way. She she said, 'Why don't you ask Yak? He is lazy but very strong and he doesn't mind being dirty. I'm sure he would help you.' She wrinkled her nose as she remembered Yak's smell.

The traders thanked Buffalo and went to find Yak.

They could smell Yak from far off. He looked strong and healthy so they held their noses while they asked him if he could help.

Yak was very pleased to be asked. He thought it would be a fine adventure. Being a greedy fellow, he said, with a glint in his eye, 'I'll help you, but at a price.'

'We'll feed you well,' they said, 'and you will be rewarded once we reach Tibet. Perhaps you should borrow a coat to keep warm up in the cold, snow-covered mountains.'

Yak thought and thought.
Who could he ask to lend him a coat?
He was conceited and smelly
so he didn't have any close friends.

One of the traders remembered the splendid coat worn by Buffalo and said, 'Buffalo has a very fine coat. Why don't you ask her to lend it to you?'

Yak trotted off in search of Buffalo and found her wallowing in the pond. Only her head was showing above the water.

Buffalo wasn't too happy to be disturbed but, being very polite, she climbed out, shook herself and asked Yak what he wanted. She was horrified when Yak said he wanted to borrow her coat. She didn't know how to reply so all she said was, 'Yak, I'm sorry but I can't lend you my coat. Please ask someone else.'

Yak walked away. He wondered who else he could ask. His adventure wasn't going to be such a fine one if it meant he would be cold.

He turned round and saw Buffalo watching him, so he lowered his head and pretended to cry. He thought *Buffalo is so kind-hearted, she can't bear to see others in trouble. Perhaps if I go back and flatter and plead, maybe then she will lend me her coat.*

'Dear Buffalo, gentle Buffalo, everyone knows you are the kindest of animals. I know the traders first asked you to help them, but you refused so I've been given the job. You would hate me to be cold so please lend me your warm coat.'

Buffalo had never heard Yak make such a long speech before. She was rather touched, so she tried to be tactful. She said, 'Yak, I understand how keen you are to take this job but I look after my coat very carefully and wash it every day. Quite honestly I don't think you are so careful. I don't believe you ever take a bath and that is probably why you haven't any close friends. I don't think you would look after my coat, especially up in the high, cold mountains where all the water has turned to ice and snow.'

Bully boy Yak kept on and on and eventually persuaded kind, gentle Buffalo to part with her coat.

He had a bit of trouble putting on the coat.

Then he looked at his reflection in the water. The coat nearly came to the ground and hung in a ruff over his neck. He thought he looked very smart and it certainly felt very cosy and warm. He was so proud and said to himself, *'Bos grunniens,'* (because that is his scientific name,) 'you are extremely intelligent and clever to have borrowed Buffalo's coat!'

Buffalo reminded him that she had only lent him her coat, not given it to him and he was to bring it back as soon as possible.

As Yak trotted away with the coat-tails swinging, he looked back over his shoulder and shouted that he promised to return her coat the following Spring.

The traders were pleased to see Yak in his borrowed coat. The next morning they tied their barrels, brass pots and boxes, rolls of cloth, tools and carpets to Yak's back with ropes. Yak was a bit nervous and wondered how he would climb with all that weight on his back. The traders were also carrying heavy loads so he dared not complain.

They set off through the foothills. It was still quite warm and Yak got very hot and sticky in Buffalo's coat. The flies buzzed around him and he thought how nice it would be to wander into a deep pond to cool off or to be living the carefree life enjoyed by his wild cousins, the *Bos mutus*, who lived in the hills.

It was hard work climbing the rough mountain tracks. Yak looked forward to the evenings when the load would be taken off his back. Then he could eat, drink and lie down to sleep and dream.

The traders were keen to get home and never took a day off to rest.
Early every morning they strapped the load onto Yak's back again and
led him on up the mountain.

In a few days they had climbed so high that even trees couldn't grow and it was far too high for any flies. They all had to move more slowly because the air was thin and they got out of breath very easily. There was nothing to eat and it was very cold and windy. Yak was so grateful for his thick, warm coat.

Higher and higher they climbed. The views were beautiful but Yak was too tired and hungry to appreciate them. He wanted to reach the pass and start on the downhill part of the journey.

They came to where snow lay on the ground. As it got thicker Yak had to put his hooves deep down through the snow to reach the solid ground. His coat-tails became wet and straggly from being dragged in the snow. Yak struggled to move forward and they made slow progress.

When they finally reached the pass through the top of the mountains Yak was feeling very sorry for himself. He looked down into Tibet but the view was hazy and he was too exhausted to ask questions. He had never had to work so hard. The traders were happy to be close to getting back home so they tried to make Yak go faster. All he wanted to do was to get rid of his heavy load, get some food into his tummy and sleep.

At last they finished descending the mountain tracks and entered the vast plains of Tibet.

After Yak's load was removed he looked around in astonishment. All around him was grass – grass in front of him, grass to the sides of him and grass behind him. He had never seen such fine grass. He had never tasted such delicious grass. Yak was so happy as he started to eat.

Yak completely forgot his promise to Buffalo that he would return her coat. He looked up at the cold, snow-covered mountains and told himself that he would never go back up there again. So poor Buffalo's coat got dirtier and dirtier and hung off him in tangled clumps. Yak didn't care. He decided he was going to stay on the grassy plains in Tibet and live happily ever after.

The Tibetans were happy that Yak stayed with them for they were able to use some of the wool from his coat to spin and weave into warm clothing and blankets.

Buffalo waited for Yak to come back over the mountains the following Spring but he didn't appear. Buffalo knew she shouldn't have trusted Yak but actually she is much more comfortable without her coat, especially in the long, hot summers when she can enjoy wallowing in the cool water without worrying about her appearance when she finally emerges.

Sometimes, when she licks her calf, Buffalo is reminded of her lost coat and wonders if Yak will bring it back. She stretches out her nose, sniffing to check whether he is coming. Then she remembers how awful he smelt and how the flies buzzed about him so she is now content to live very happily without a coat.

Lightning Source UK Ltd.
Milton Keynes UK
UKRC02n1256220918
329330UK00005B/76